Mousetropolis

R. Gregory Christie

| City Mouse | Country Mouse |

Holiday House / New York

For Daniella Chace,
thank you for the kindness and friendship

Library of Congress Cataloging-in-Publication Data
Christie, R. Gregory, 1971- author, illustrator.
Mousetropolis / by R. Gregory Christie. — First edition.
pages cm
Summary: In this update of the classic fable, City Mouse and his cousin, Country Mouse,
exchange visits and, although they find many things to like in each other's homes,
they quickly learn that each prefers his own.
ISBN 978-0-8234-2319-4 (hardcover)
[1. Fables. 2. Mice—Folklore.] I. Country mouse and the city mouse. II. Title.
PZ8.2.C55Mou 2015
[E]—dc23
2013020212

Too much noise!

In the wee hours of the morning in downtown Mousetropolis, City Mouse was wide-awake.

He needed a vacation.

What luck! A letter came
from Country Mouse.

Quicker than a mouse can nibble
through a wedge of Cheddar, City
Mouse was in the country . . .

and sitting down to his first country
meal of rice, beans and barley.
"Uh, not for me," City Mouse said.
"So what do you do for fun?"

"This seems dangerous,"
City Mouse said.
"It is," said his
country cousin.
"Keep walking."

At the jamboree,
City Mouse and
Country Mouse
danced . . .

and played music.
"Not bad," said City Mouse.

But going home . . .

City Mouse felt as if he was being watched.
And he was.

Later that night it was too hot and too quiet.

City Mouse and Country Mouse had the same idea.

The cousins hurried toward the train and . . .

The train pulled in.

"Home," said City Mouse.

At the station there was music
and dancing everywhere.

Busy mice did important things.

And there was lots to eat.

But . . .

Quicker than a mouse can nibble through a wheel of provolone, Country Mouse was back in the country.

"Home," said
Country Mouse.

"Home," said City Mouse.